DIFFERENT, NOT DUMB

 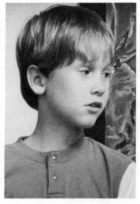   

BY MARGOT MAREK   Photographs by Barbara Kirk

 Franklin Watts   New York/London/Toronto/Sydney   1985

**For Elizabeth and Alexander,
who helped me to learn**

Library of Congress Cataloging in Publication Data

Marek, Margot.
    Different, not dumb.

    Summary: Because he gets some letters mixed up
or reversed, Mike is assigned to a special class in
which he learns the basic reading skills he eventually
uses to avert a serious accident.
    1. Children's stories, American. [1. Reading—
Fiction   2. Dyslexia—Fiction.   3. Schools—Fiction]
I. Kirk, Barbara, ill.   II. Title.
PZ7.M3352Di 1985   [E]   84-21900
ISBN 0-531-04722-9

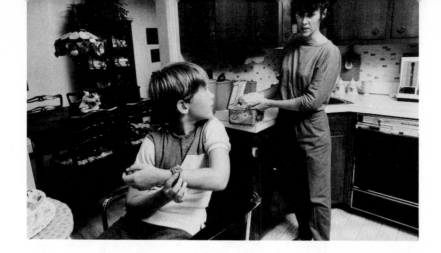

Mike was eating his breakfast. "What time is it, Mom?" he asked. He didn't want to be late for school.

"Where is the small hand on the clock?" she called back. She was packing Mike's lunchbox.

"It's between seven and eight," Mike said.

"And the big hand?"

"At the eight."

"Then it's twenty to eight," she said. "You have only five minutes till you have to go."

Mike ate the last bite of toast. He wished he could tell time by himself. It should have been easy for him. He liked numbers. He could add and subtract. But he still got mixed up about telling time. It was just one more thing that was making him feel dumb now. Second grade was just beginning, but most of the kids knew how to read, too. He began to worry about school.

"I think I have a sore throat, Mom," Mike said.

She came over and put her hand on his forehead. "No fever," she said. "Take a drink of orange juice."

Mike drank the juice. His mother looked at him. She seemed to know how he felt. But she just said, "Now get your jacket and go out to wait for the bus. I love you, Mike."

He shut the front door and jumped down the steps. He ran across the yard and climbed up on the fence. He had learned to balance there for a minute before he had to jump down. He hoped Jeff could see him from the school bus.

"Hi, Mike," Jeff called. "Come sit here." Mike felt good sitting next to his best friend. "That's a good trick," Jeff said.

"I'll teach it to you after school."

Mike sat at his desk. He listened to the teacher.

"Write your name on the *left* side of your paper," Miss Parker said. "Then number the paper from one to ten. Copy the spelling words from the blackboard."

Mike looked for the little scar that told him which was his left hand. He didn't hear the next thing she said.

"What did she say, Jeff?" he asked.

"Write your name . . ."

"I heard that."

"Then write the numbers from one to ten."

"Mike, Jeff! You won't know what to do if you are talking," Miss Parker scolded.

Jeff turned away from Mike. It seemed to Mike that Jeff was mad at him, too. Suddenly he couldn't sit still any more. He got up and went to look at the goldfish. Miss Parker came over and put her hand on his shoulder.

"Come back to your desk, Mike. I'll show you what to do."

In a way Mike liked that. He wanted to do it right. But he wanted to be able to do it himself.

He copied the first word, then the next. Jeff looked at his paper.

"You wrote f-e-l-t instead of l-e-f-t," he said. Mike rubbed hard to erase the mistake. He tried again. He looked at Jeff's paper to make sure. Jeff had already copied all ten words. Mike was only up to number four.

"Get ready for reading, now, children," Miss Parker said. "Red group, read the story and then answer the questions."

Jeff was in the red group. Mike knew they were the best. They didn't even need the teacher. The blue group was all right, too. Miss Parker got them started. A girl from sixth grade was there to help them.

"Now yellow group, let's get ready," Miss Parker said. Mike got a funny feeling in his chest. He got it every time he had to read. Slowly he carried his chair to the circle.

"We are on page ten," Miss Parker said. Mike listened to Tom reading. Tom was his friend, too.

"The po . . . the pol . . ."

"The policeman," Miss Parker said.

"The policeman . . . saw . . . the dog."

"Good, Tom. It's your turn, Mike."

Mike turned the page. He saw a word beginning with "d." Or was it "b"? He took a chance. "The boy ran."

Tom laughed. "Shut up," Mike said.

The teacher said, "The *dog* ran." She looked at Mike. "You knew that word yesterday and the day before, Mike." She seemed mad and sad at the same time. It made him feel mad and sad, too.

That afternoon Miss Parker gave Mike a note to take home. He forgot about it while he and Jeff balanced on the fence. He didn't remember it until after supper.

His mother and father read the note together. "What does it say?" Mike asked. "I was bad in reading today. Do I have to go back to first grade?" He was really scared.

"Oh, no, Mike, not that." His father hugged him. "They just want to test you. To find out why you have trouble reading."

"What if I don't do it right? Then will I have to go back to first grade?"

He was still scared the day of the test. Maybe his Mom and Dad didn't really know what would happen.

The testing room was small. The test lady smiled. "Come in, Mike," she said. "We have lots to do."

Two hours went by. There were puzzles to do and blocks to fit into patterns. Mike had to say the alphabet and name the days of the week. There was a little bit about letters and words. There were even some numbers to add. "That's easy," Mike said.

"Easy for you," the lady answered. "That's what I'm finding out. What is easy for you and what is hard. Everyone is better at some things. Everyone needs help with other things."

Mike shook his head. "I'm just not good at school. I never will be."

"Wait and see, Mike," she said. "You *do* need help with reading. Then you will catch up. You aren't dumb, you know."

Mike looked at her hard. He wanted to believe
her. He began to hope that she was right. Maybe he
just needed some help.

The help came from Miss Kent, the special reading teacher. Every day, for part of playground time, Mike and Tom and Jill went to Miss Kent's room.

"Miss Kent's reading group, line up at the door," the teacher said. Mike got up slowly and stood next to Jill. He saw Jeff looking at him. "I bet he thinks I'm dumb, too," Mike thought. Everyone knew Miss Kent's group was dumb.

"See you in the playground," Jeff whispered. "I'll save you a swing."

Mike felt a little better, thinking about going outside. He always felt pretty smart outside. He even felt good in Miss Kent's room now.

She had told them that there were many ways to learn to read. Some children learn by seeing the words over and over again.

That's how they did it in the classroom. Other children need a different way. Miss Kent said she would teach them the sound of each letter. Then she would teach them how to put the letters together. "Words have rules," she said. "You have to learn them." And Mike did.

Now he knew the sounds the letters made. After a while he could tell "b" from "d." Miss Kent's books had words he could figure out. Now he could *read* the words, not just guess.

One day there was a little puzzle at his place. It was shaped like a train and it had a word on it. The train came apart into two pieces. The word came apart, too.

"What does your word say?" Miss Kent asked.

Mike put the train together. The word looked too long. "I don't know," he said.

"Take it apart again."

Mike did. He saw "him" on one piece. "Him . . . something," he said.

"Look at the other piece. See if you can sound it out."

" 'S,' " he said. " 'S-s-s.' Then 'e' like egg. Then 'l.' That makes 'sel.' "

"And the 'f'? " Miss Kent asked.

"Sel-f . . . self!" Mike shouted.

"Now put the train together again."

"Him . . . self," Mike said slowly. "It says himself! And I got it by *my*self. How do you spell my?" Mike asked.

Miss Kent smiled and told him.

Mike wrote "my" and "self" together. "Look, Jill, I made 'myself.' "

Jill looked. "It's 's-e-l-f,' " Jill said. "You have 's-l-e-f.' "

"Oh well," Mike said. "Nobody's perfect."

After class, Mike ran out to the playground. Jeff was on top of the jungle gym. "Come on up, Mike," he yelled. They pretended they were flying a rocket. Mike leaned way out, holding on with one hand.

Mike saw a red truck going along the road next to the playground. It went over a bump.

"Look, Jeff. Something fell off that red truck. Let's go see what it is."

They ran to the end of the playground. They saw a big box at the side of the road. It had a funny picture on it. It had a very long word, too. Jeff tried to pick up the box.

"Wait!" Mike said. "What does it say, Jeff?"

"I don't know," Jeff said. "That word is too long for me. I've never seen it before. Ex . . . ex-something."

"Break it up into little bits," Mike said. "That's what we do in Miss Kent's room."

"Hey, that's smart," Jeff said. "I usually just know the whole word. This time I'll try it your way."

"Hurry," Mike said.

"Ex . . . plo. Explos . . . explosives!" Jeff shouted. He jumped away from the box.

"Help," Mike said. "We'd better tell Miss Parker."

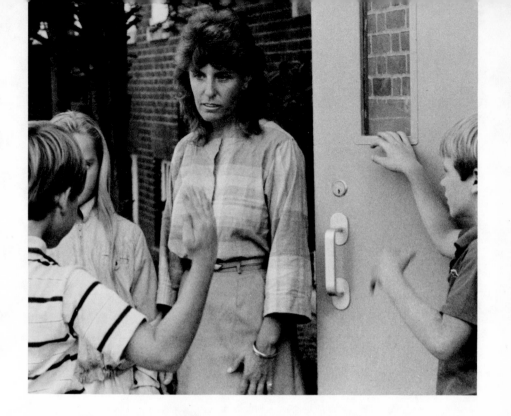

The boys ran back to the playground. The children were in line to go back to class. "Where have you two been?" Miss Parker began.

Mike and Jeff both talked at once.

"We saw a truck."

"And a box fell off."

"And we were going to pick it up."

"But it said 'explosives.' "

"We'd better get out of here!"

"Wait," Miss Parker said. "Are you sure that is the word? It's a hard word even for you, Jeff."

"I'm sure," Jeff said. "Mike told me to break it up, and then I could read it."

"Wait here, all of you," Miss Parker said. When she came back, she looked a little bit scared, too. "Let's go inside, children. Jeff and Mike are right. It does say 'explosives.' I've called the police to take care of it."

Later, a policeman came into the classroom. "Where are the two boys who found the box?" he asked.

Miss Parker called Mike and Jeff to her desk.

"You boys are really heroes," the policeman said. "Someone might have been badly hurt. Explosives isn't an easy word. You must be the best readers, too."

Mike started to explain. But Jeff just looked at him and winked. "Together we are," he said.